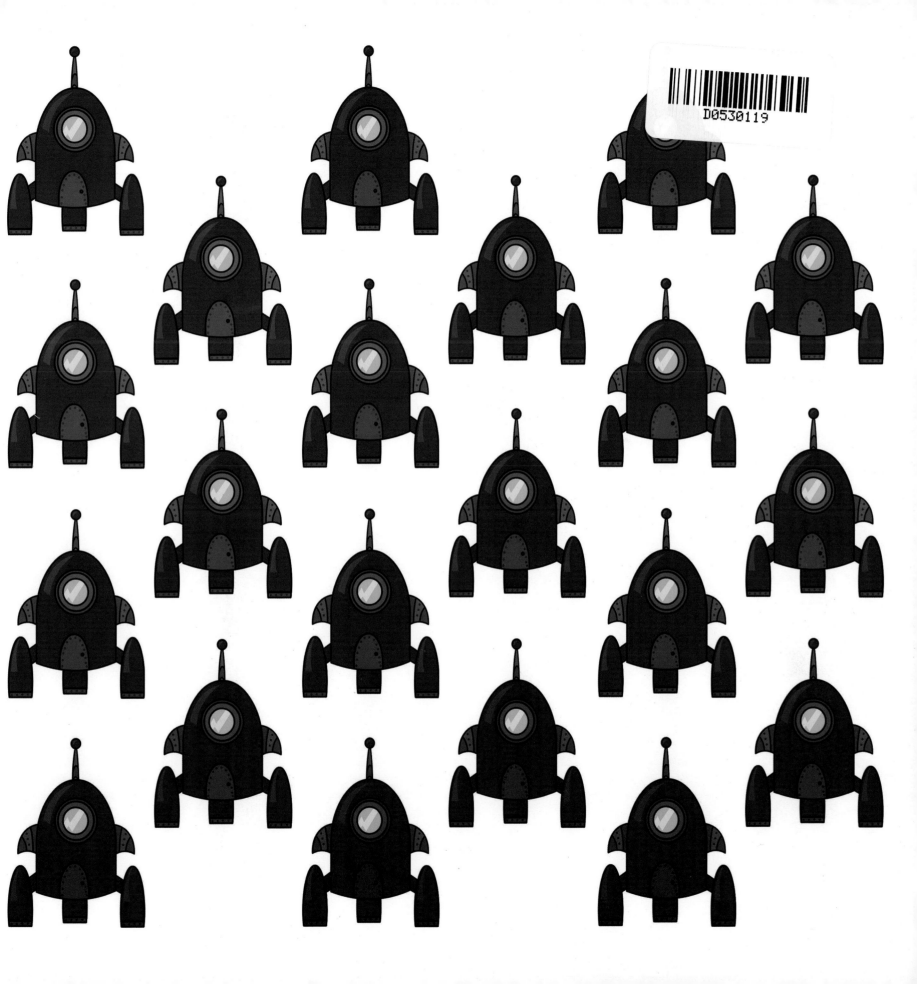

*For Sam*

First published in 2017 by Rockpool Children's Books Ltd.

This edition published in 2017 by Rockpool Children's Books Ltd.
in association with Albury Books.
Albury Court, Albury, Tha me
OX9 2LP, United Kingdom

Text and Illustrations copyright © Simon Partington 2017

Simon Partington has asserted the moral rights
to be identified as the author and illustrator of this book.
© Rockpool Children's Books Ltd. 2017

Printed in China

ISBN 978-1-906081-95-9 (Paperback)

**rockpool**
children's books

Albury Books

Simon Partington

# The Funny Little Moon Man

## A Very Special Visitor!

Sam looked at the moon through his telescope and was very surprised to see someone looking back at him.

Up in space, the funny little moon man looked at the sparkling blue and green planet and was very surprised to see someone looking back at him!

"Hmmm," thought Sam. "I should go there one day."

He looked at his rocket made from cardboard boxes and tin foil. "I'm not sure this would get me all the way to the moon," he thought.

"Hmmm," thought the
funny little moon man.
"I should go there one day."
He looked at his
little red rocket.
The hull gleamed in the
bright sunshine and the
engines hummed
quietly.

The door closed and the funny little moon man shouted "5, 4, 3, 2, 1!" He hit a big red button...

**WHAP!**

...and the little red rocket began to tremble.

"Little Red Rocket go, go, go!"
cheered
the funny little moon man,
and the rocket took off with a

*WHOOOSH!*

Sam was playing in his bedroom when he heard a loud rumbling noise. He looked through his telescope and was amazed to see a little red rocket making its way towards the garden.

The little red rocket landed in a cloud of steam and dust, with a BUMP.

"Hello!"
said the funny little
moon man.
"Hello!" said Sam.

"Come on in,"
said the funny little
moon man.

"Wow," said Sam. "This is amazing."
Lights flashed and twinkled,
and beeps beeped and buzzed.
"Strap yourself in Sam,"
said the funny little moon man.
"We're going for a ride."

The door closed and
the funny little moon man
shouted
"5, 4, 3, 2, 1!"
He hit a big red button...

**WHAP!**

and the little red rocket

**WHOOOSHED**

into the sky.

Sam saw the world beneath him disappear and the two travellers were soon cruising through space.

Sam watched through the windows excitedly and was amazed to see a family of **shooting stars,** who waved as the little red rocket dashed past them. The rocket took a sharp left and dropped quickly, making Sam's tummy feel funny.

They were heading for the
moon and Sam whooped gleefully
as they rushed along the valley floors,
scattering **moon sheep**
as they went.

"That was amazing," cheered Sam. "If you liked that, you'll love this," said the funny little moon man.

The rocket blasted off high into space; and Sam watched as the moon disappeared from sight.

Space went very quiet for a few moments, but then Sam saw a most incredible sight.
**"Pluto!"** squealed the funny little moon man excitedly.
"And the cactus tickle," he chuckled.

As they whooshed down to the surface Sam was sure he could hear the little red rocket giggling as the cactus plants tickled it. The little red rocket squirmed and jiggled this way and that, making Sam and the funny little moon man shriek with laughter.

"Show me more, show me more," shouted Sam. The funny little moon man smiled kindly and said, "Not today, it's nearly teatime".

The little red rocket whooshed off again. **"Little Red Rocket go, go, go!"** cheered the funny little moon man and - in a flash - they were on their way to Sam's house.

"Thank you for a wonderful trip," said Sam.
"You're welcome," said the funny little moon man.
"Will I see you again?" asked Sam
"Oh yes," said the funny little moon man.
"I'm sure I'll need your help very soon!"

The little red rocket
took off with a

**WHOOOSH**

and Sam smiled as his new
friend disappeared into
the stars shouting,
**"Little red rocket,
go, go, go!"**

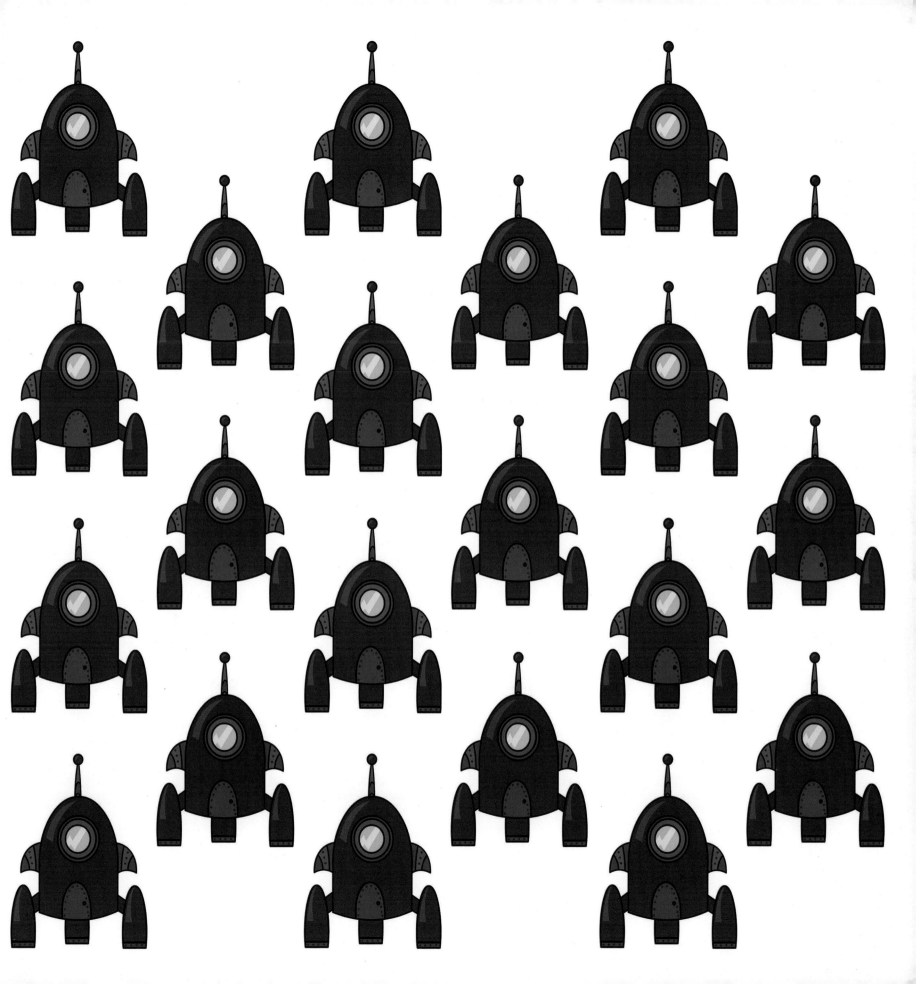

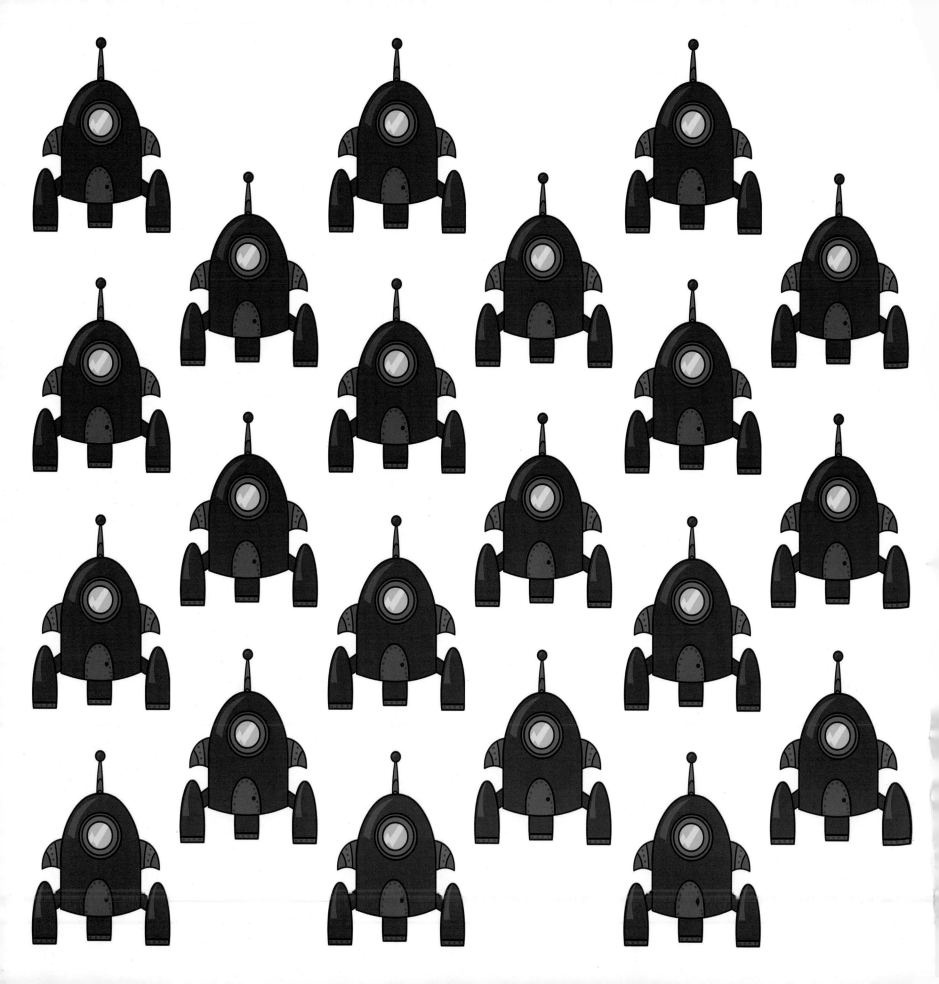